I0714420

THE YOUNG AND THE OLD

THE YOUNG AND THE OLD

by Paul Sutton

Photographs by Paul Sutton

Drawings by Paul Dufficey

Buffalo Books

THE YOUNG AND THE OLD

All text and photographs © Paul Sutton, 2015
Line Art © Paul Dufficey, 2015

'The Old Man' was previously published in
the Cambridge University journal *Imponderabilia*

Are 'Friends' Electric picture disc © Gary Numan/WEA

Paul Sutton is identified as the author of this book.
The moral rights of the author have been asserted.

First hardback edition (January 2015)
ISBN: 978-0-9572462-9-4

First paperback edition (February 2015)
ISBN: 978-0-9931770-0-2

camerajournal@hotmail.com

All rights reserved. No part of this publication may be reproduced, stored in a retrieval system or transmitted in any form or by any means electronic, mechanical, photocopying, recording, print on demand or otherwise, without the prior written permission of the author. This book is sold subject to the condition that it shall not, by way of trade or otherwise, be lent, re-sold, hired out or otherwise circulated without the publisher's prior consent in any form of binding or cover other than that in which it is published and without a similar condition including this condition being imposed on the subsequent purchaser

Published by Buffalo Books, Cambridge

Also by Paul Sutton:

The Moving Picture Boy Gallery
Six English Filmmakers
Becoming Ken Russell
Lindsay Anderson, The Diaries
if.... A British Film Guide

Coming soon:
The Moving Picture Girl Gallery
Conversations with Six English Film Directors
Charlie Ellis, The Three Journeys (a novel)

For Maureen Thulin
without whom...

Illustrations

Stories

The Captain

Angels Pre-School

The Captain of the ship was stubborn and exacting. He set the boundaries. He set the rules. It wasn't wise to cross him or to question him. Having little regard for his contemporaries, he was happiest when alone and would tolerate the presence of others only if they were much older than himself. His emotions were extreme. He could scream like a madman and cry like a girl. Most of the time, his face was locked in a look of unapproachable thoughtfulness; his high brow dark with creases, his breathing deep and measured. But he had a musical laugh, a surprisingly high-pitched giggle and a watery mouth which sometimes dribbled.

His favourite playmate was a teenage girl, not quite twenty, who helped with the playgroup on Wednesdays. He tolerated her because she knew not to attempt to take control. "There," said the Captain, pointing to a place on the floor where the girl had to sit to be on board the ship. She did as she was told. The Captain returned his attention to looking for the key.

"Can I help you to find it?" asked the girl. "What does it look like?". The Captain had made the key by using long leaves to bind two twigs. He thought he'd brought it inside when it started to rain. "Is it a magic key?" asked the girl, careful not to hurry him. Hurrying him would fluster him. Flustering meant tears. The difference between a sea voyage and a tantrum was very small.

"If it's a magic key it might be invisible?"

The Captain didn't answer. His unblinking eyes scoured the room.

"I've got a key, here," she said, digging a hand into her pocket and bringing out her front door key. The Captain was momentarily impressed. He liked the shiny metal but the key wasn't the right shape.

The young woman tried her luck with: "Do pirate ships need a key to start them?" and was scalded with a look of severe disgust. "It's not a pirate ship," he said. "It's a spaceship."

"I'm sorry. I didn't know — Can we make another key?"

The Captain paused and nodded.

"What do we make it from?"

"Sticks."

The girl looked around for something that looked like sticks and, without getting to her feet, found a wooden ruler.

"Will this do?"

The Captain nodded.

She gave him the ruler.

"Two," said the Captain.

She looked for and found another ruler.

Cross-legged, now with a ruler in each hand, the Captain touched one ruler with the other.

"Do we need to bind them together?

"Together," said the Captain, letting the rulers fall to the floor.

The girl looked around for something to bind the rulers. She got to her feet. From a cupboard, she took a packet of elastic bands. She took them to the Captain and sat down. She said: "Can I have the rulers, please?"

The Captain gave her the rulers, one at a time.

"Thank you."

He looked closely as she looped and locked them together with elastic. But it wasn't right.

"What's the matter with it?" asked the girl.

The Captain didn't answer. His face started to darken.

"Have I done it wrong?" said the girl, taking the rulers back. "What shape should it be?"

The Captain tried to articulate what he wanted. He wanted one stick upwards and one stick across.

"Like this?"

The Captain nodded. She fixed the rulers into the shape of a cross. The Captain used the key-cross to start the engine of the spaceship,--- then he placed it in its proper place on the ground at his feet. He pushed it gently this way and that way to make sure it was in the right place.

"Belt," he said looking up to her, over his shoulder.

The girl didn't understand.

"Belt!' demanded the Captain.

"Seatbelt?"

The Captain nodded.

She knelt forward and mimed placing a seatbeat around him. He lifted up his arm so she could fit it properly to his seat.

"I'll put my belt on now," she said, sitting back down and miming the fixing of her own seatbelt. Satisfied that everything was in order, the Captain made the noise of a gentle but powerful take-off and, when they were in space, the girl said to him: "Where are we going?"

The Captain didn't answer.

"Is it going to be nice when we get there?"

"Yes."

"What's nice about it?"

He didn't answer.

"Will there be animals there?"

He didn't answer.

"Flowers?"

He didn't answer.

Looking for clues she looked around the classroom at the
pictures on the walls. His paintings were of rainbows. There
were churches and people and rainbows.

"Are there rainbows there?"

The Captain nodded.

"You like painting rainbows, don't you?"
He nodded.

His Grandad had gone away and everyone at home was very
sad. His mother told him that Grandad had gone to a nice
place in the stars and was happy there, and was no longer ill.

"Grandad's a rainbow," said the boy. His eyes started to fill.

The Farm

The man was five-times older than the boy who, at eight years old, had taken it on himself to make sure that the man was safe during his extended stay on the farm. The man was from a foreign country and was not used to life on a farm. The boy knew this from the man's clothes, which were quite unsuitable for the dirt and dust difficulties of farm life. When the workers were castrating the new bulls, the boy made sure the man stood away from the fence when the boys opened the gate to the corral and drove the nervous bulls inside. He did this gently by showing the man the proper hand-foot-hand-foot way to get down from the high fence. And when they had both got down from the fence, the boy said: "You need to step back. You need to step away from the fence."

The man did as he was told.

When the farmer's knife came out, the man said: "You don't need to see this bit." And he tried to cover the boy's eyes, but the boy stepped away and said: "It doesn't bother me. I've seen it lots of times already. I saw it first when I was five."

The bulls did make the most awful sound.

The boy asked the man: "What sound did you think cows made before you came here?"

The man said: "Moo."

"Now you know the truth," said the boy. With a concentrated seriousness, the boy then demonstrated the three distinct noises of real bulls and real cows.

And now the man and the boy were walking to the lake in the middle of the farm. It's a big lake, clean and stocked with spiky sport-fish for catching and eating. But they didn't fish. They skimmed stones. The boy's best was seven. The man bettered the seven by seven.

On the walk home, they walked with a bend in their spine and hand on their hip and they talked in voices that sounded like they were Mid-Western old-timers.

"I remember when injuns used to come up here all a-hollerin' and makin' mischief," said the man.

"Old Black Hawk sure was one mean old man," said the boy, hunched over, and talking with an old man's voice. "But he was smart."

"Been here longer than us. Knew the land better than us. Gotta give him that."

The boy unstooped briefly to pick up a stick and use it as a walking-stick. Now he walked along with one hand on his side and one hand on the stick. It took some effort not to break character and use the stick to hit loose stones. "But I'm so old, I remember when Black Hawk was born. Cried like a baby he did." The boy did the wah-wah cry of a newborn.

"I remember his papa bein' born," said the man, and that made the boy laugh.

When the boy was done laughing, the man said: "You see that barn?"

"I do," said the boy, in an old man's voice, stretching out the vowels.

"I built that barn with these fair hands."

"Those cottonwood trees," said the boy. "Planted 'em all. Tiny seeds, but a lot of diggin'. Yes, sir!"

"'Pressive. Grown good. That hill though," said the man raising his head to a small hill behind the farmhouse. "Made it mostly from earth I moved to build the house. We worked hard in those days."

"We worked good," said the boy.

They walked for a long time without talking.

Screams

The fairground came to town at the dog-end of winter and parked within a phalanx of caravans and trucks on wasteland in the foothills of slag-heaps that rose beyond the Eastern border. The only building in this part of town was a brown-tiled and towered windowless Art Deco folly, a members only Conservative Club. It served the cheapest drinks in town but locked its doors for the fair's duration. There were almost no street-lights in this part of town, which is how the travellers liked it. They brought their own lights. The travellers lights lit up the night sky and danced on the underside of clouds. The travellers also brought pop music amplified from speakers, erected on poles protected by barbed wire, and played at a volume so loud that the bass thumped mile after mile across town, beating inside children's chests and bringing them in in their hundreds. Parentless for the night, the town-children met inside the phalanx in groups of twos and threes and fours, their pockets ringing with coins to spend.

The most popular rides were the most dangerous, the ones which could maim and could kill, and which did. Every third year someone would fall from the spinning cages which circled within rising and falling circles, or someone's arm or leg would be ripped away, caught in the gap between the ride and the steps on the thrilling spinning Speedway (whisper it, the steps are painted red). Almost all the rides were hydraulic spinning machines, hand-painted with pop-art images of Elvis Presley, Star Wars, Marilyn Monroe. In this part of the world, a portrait on the side of a fairground ride meant more than a star on the Hollywood Walk. The stars were usually

American, but — "Look at that!". In paint, the talk of the playground: blank-faced zombies with glowing eyes and white spiky hair, and a black-shirted man, arms crossed in a theatrical pose, his eyes ringed with mascara, his head pierced by wires. The images were of a new popular singer, and an advert for jeans which had the refrain: "Don't be a Dummy! Use your Money!". The singer's thin nasal London voice was the very essence of punk rock, sneeringly confident, but somehow also sounding fragile and wounded.

The machines turned. The music played. Children screamed.

Preparation

Summer had come round again. The oldest boys had moved on. Bred to serve, they had taken the next step up on the ladder of their vocation. There were some new boys; one new master; and some old faces. The tents were being loaded onto the flat back lorry. Leading the loading was an oldish man with skinny legs and knobble-knee shorts and weather-browned arms, a popular man who did all the manual labour on the camp, including the digging and the maintenance of the latrines. The boys called him 'Bog Arthur', which they sang to the tune of 'Blackadder'. The boys spent their time, between the lifting and the tying, throwing a ball around. Their ability to transcend age differences, so that they all were one group, was good to see. One of the boys accidentally hit the new master in the chest with the ball and, for an instant, recoiled with imagined repercussions, for the new master was too new into adulthood to be quite sure that this was not a moment for asserting his authority. But the ball came back without a flinch or a word and the game continued.

Two of the younger boys had skived off work and were hiding under a boat. "We're checking it for holes," they said when challenged by the new master. He told them to go with him to the swimming pool to fetch the accessories for the canoes. One of the boys handed him a dossier he had written about "pond life found in the swimming pool".

"You're exaggerating."

"I'm not, Sir."

It was true that the pool needed a good clean. The building which housed it, a fifties prefab with a corrugated roof, was also in need of repair. The water was covered by a blue canvas sheet that was said to keep the heat in, but it was there really to keep the boys out. It was rumoured that one of them had managed to run across it.

"Don't exaggerate."

"I saw him."

"Who?"

The boy blushed in answer. He'd rather die than tell.

Bog Arthur had finished tying down a canvas cover and had turned his and the boys' attention to the first of the four minibuses.

"I'm not going with Dr. Trotter. He drives like a madman."

"You'll go with who you're told," said Bog Arthur.

"I hope I'm with Major Tomkinson."

Everyone liked Major Tomkinson, except for the fact he was never without a lit cigar. He would slap down a fifty-pound note on the counter of the motorway café and say: "There's my fine. Now don't moan if I smoke."

Oliver, whom everyone called 'Ollie', and who, in time, would lead one of the patrols, announced he would never go into battle because he was far too good-looking.

"Who told you you were good-looking?"

"My girlfriends."

(He would die in battle).

Ollie greeted one of the late arrivals with a grin and a "My, it's good of you to join us". The boy's mother apologised for her son's lateness but not for his appearance. He was wearing a red Hawaiian shirt, the loudness of which made the new master wince. Another late arriver, Alex, looked tired and a little worried. He walked off with his parents, talking all the while while his parents listened. He wasn't a boy one ordinarily worried about. The new master made a mental note.

'recoiled with imagined repercussions'

Safe

She didn't have a coat because she didn't need a coat. She didn't have waterproof shoes because she didn't need waterproof shoes. She didn't have an umbrella though it rained four days in ten. But they bought her a mobile phone to make her safe. They said: "We'll be able to reach her wherever she is. It'll make her safe." But this made no sense, because they wouldn't let her leave the house on her own. "It's better to be safe than sorry. When you are eighteen you can do whatever you want. But as long as you live here you live by our rules." Their rules were writ from a fear that strangled the bond called love. "It's for your own good. Yes, I know. Yes, I know. But it was different then. Things were different back then."

(There was trust).

Each day, in the four quarters, they drove her to school and back, bumper-to-bumpered safe in a four-by-four in their low-lying gridlocked hill-less town. And the girl tumbled down into the secret worlds of the telephone, a wonderland warren where truth wasn't a virtue. Where virtue wasn't a virtue. And where time ran by like a white rabbit. Late. She was admired from Delhi to Doncaster. A popularity grown from need and standing on the weakest foundation.

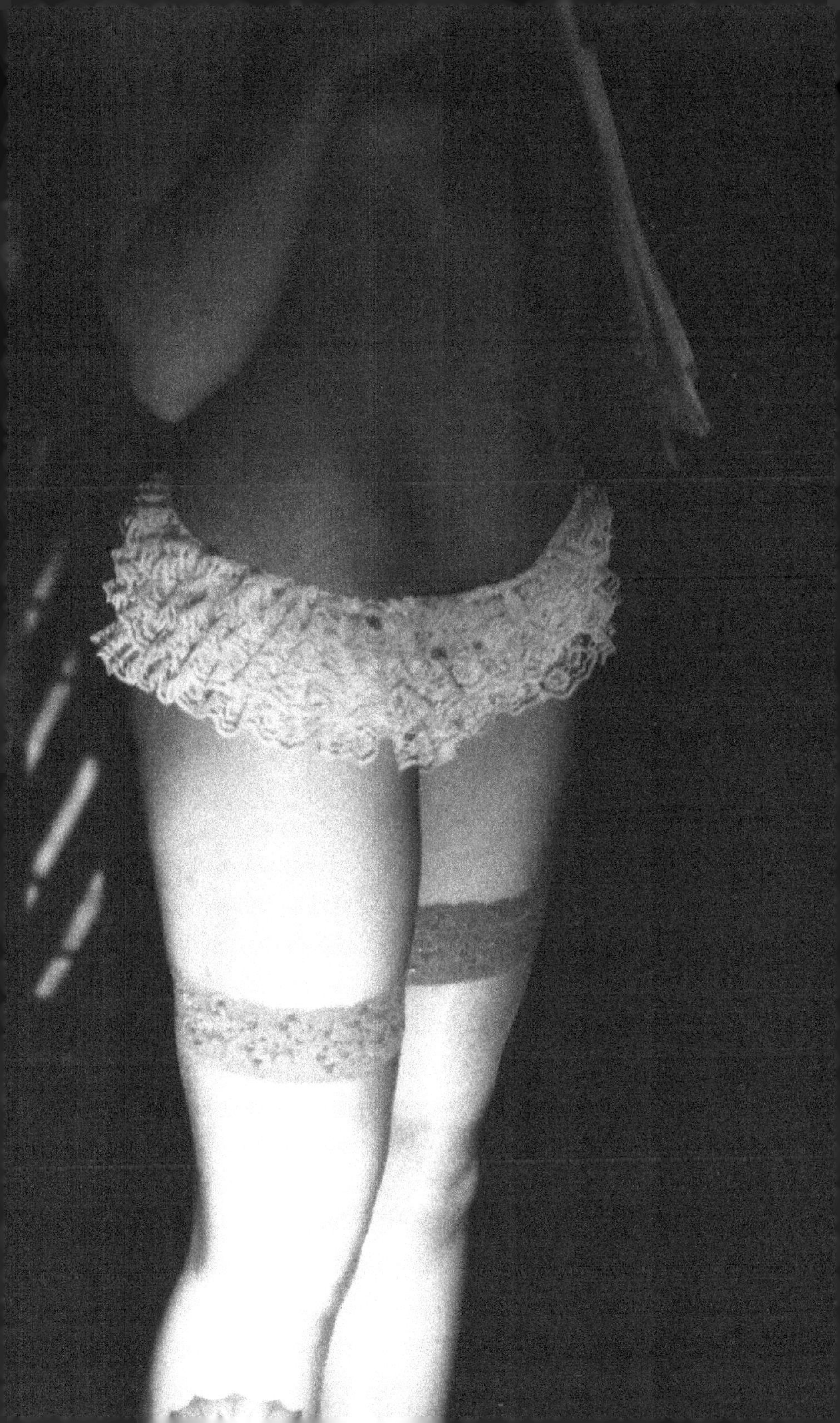

A Tight Fitting Dress

It was a time before the internet, and he was too young to buy the top-shelf magazines which he sometimes found abandoned in woodlands and by guilty roadsides, and his mental store of images was running low. He sought inspiration from the pages of the television guide and, in the smudgy black-and-white text, he found hope: a late film about a seaside holiday. New. He imagined long scenes of beautiful bodies in two-piece suits, and was sure there would be glimpses of flesh. Buttocks. Breasts. But the film proved to be a period-piece set in the 1950s when the English still went to the beach fully clothed. He continued to watch more in hope than in expectation and, as his hopes faded, his demands declined to the point where he was satisfied by the sight of a tight-fitting dress.

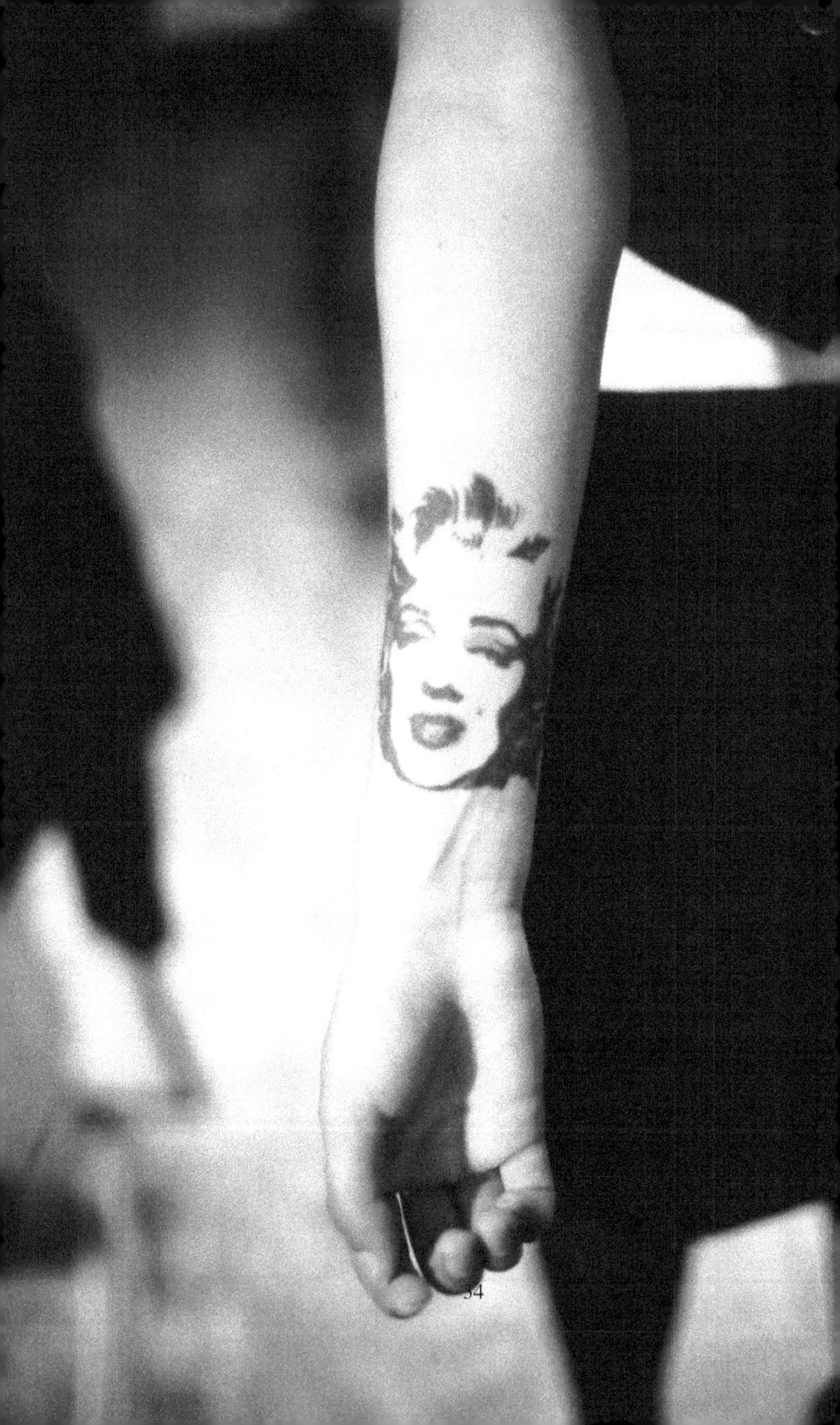

The Girl

She didn't like him.

And she didn't like *him*.

She didn't like her.

And she didn't like them.

But what she liked least of all was herself.

She hated her own face. She hated her own body. She hated her family.

"What do you not like about your family?"

"Everything."

"There's nothing about them that you like?"

"No."

"What about your mother's laugh? Your father's smile?"

"Are you mental?"

"I'm not mental. And you are not mental. You are perfectly sane. Perfectly good."

This made the girl suspicious. It stopped her from talking for quite a while.

It took many weeks before they could begin to unlock the reasons.

"Shall we start at the top? At the top of you? You told me once that you didn't like your hair."

"I hate my hair."

There were many reasons why the girl didn't like her hair. The first reason she gave was that it was the wrong colour. Worse than that, she said, it didn't really have any colour. Was it brown? or was it blonde? Some days it looked grey. That was one of the reasons why she dyed it black. The second reason she gave was that her hair never felt right.

"What do you mean by not feeling right?"

"It's not like the hair you see in magazines."

And, after a long time, the girl remembered her hair being pulled by someone from whom she was seeking love.

"How old were you then?"

"I can't remember."

'You said you didn't like your nose."

"I hate my nose."

"What's wrong with your nose?"

'Everything."

"Does it work?"

There was silence.

"Well that's something - if it works. It can't be all bad if it
works. In Italy, there's a very famous woman called Sophia
Loren. She's a bit before your time but, for many years, she
was said by many people to be the most beautiful woman
in the world. She was in all the best films and all the best
magazines. She topped all the polls. Let me show you a
picture of her. And, if you don't mind, I'll also show you a
picture of you. This is a picture of Sophia Loren. And this is
a picture of you. Please look at the pictures and tell me what
you see. Do you see what I see when I look at them?"

The girl looked at the pictures and said: "She's got the same
nose as me."

"Yes. You've got a beautiful nose."

Many years later, when the girl was now a woman and had a
daughter of her own, she was combing her young daughter's
hair lavishingly and with love. And in this moment of
contentment, she thought back to the day when her life was

changed by a kind word from a stranger. She never told anyone what the doctor had said to her. The knowledge given to her from him that her nose was beautiful was the secret store from which she drew a long lifetime of pride and comfort and hope.

The Vicar's Son

The Vicar's son was seventeen years old and he had shaved off all his hair, except for a thin layer of blond scrub which he liked to rub when he was sitting still. He said: "Type 'football hooligans' into youtube. There's some great videos on it."

I typed.

We watched.

He said: "You really get a sense of the excitement, don't you? I've been there. I've been to that place. I know that street."

On the video, three undernourished youths in polyester clothes were standing on the doorstep of a clapboard house and were proudly displaying the cover of a local newspaper which carried their arrest photographs on Page One. The photographs had been slipped to the editor, for a nominal sum, by a clerk of the court who liked to name and shame.

I turned to say something to the Vicar's son but he had stopped listening a long time ago. He was striding around the room, making exaggerated gestures and cocking his head back and forth. He was out on the street and he was loving it.

Climbing

He was a twenty-year-old white boy with gingery hair, and he was the youngest person to climb the highest mountains on the seven continents of the Earth. His enthusiasm for climbing came at the age of fourteen when, in his local scout troop, he signed up for a week of serious climbing in Scotland. There, on climbing a weather-difficult peak, he announced he would climb Everest before he was twenty. And he did. He climbed it with his own two hands and his own two feet. And he learned the meaning of fear. And he learned the meaning of cold. He learned the meaning of distance and of time. And he learned what pain was.

His achievements made the national newpapers in expensive advertisements paid for by his sponsor, whose banner he had to unfurl in the two minutes nature and the schedule allowed him to stand on the top of the world. Breathless. His record for the Seven Peaks was noted on an English postage stamp, but instead of the boy's own image, and the boy's own name, the stampmakers used a poorly painted picture of two other scout children. One of the children was black. The white child was female.

The Student

He woke late and missed the rescheduled meeting with the old Professor who taught the course on political history, though taught isn't really the right word for the Professor's method of playing tape-recordings of political speeches and asking his students to comment on them. The student had been waking late for the best part of a year. He woke late to the noise of music playing in the rooms on each side of his. Helen was playing middle-of-the-road rock. Simon was playing Bob Dylan. The student didn't like Helen's music and he didn't like Simon's and, although it woke him, and sometimes stopped him from sleeping, their music was rarely played at a wholly anti social level. The problem was that neither had the grace to mute the impact of their noise by closing their bedroom doors which stood ever open like a pair of gaping mouths. The student was one of six who shared an end-of-terrace house on a busy main road in a watery low-sky town in the middle of England. Three of the other five students had semi-permanent live-in partners. Therefore nine people shared one kitchen. Nine shared one bathroom. Six shared the bills which six couldn't really afford.

The student's room was cold so, on waking, he stayed in bed and, from the bed today, he watched a television broadcast of *Gabriel over the White House*, a crude propaganda feature film from the era of Roosevelt's New Deal. He didn't take notes.

In the mid-afternoon, the student went fruit-shopping at the market where he bought a banana and an orange for himself for each day of the coming week, plus a few extras for the others.

On returning from the market, his mood of benevolence was broken by a pile of broken biscuits on the carpeted floor of the front room. In the chair next to the discarded pile was Helen. "Are these yours?" he asked. Helen affirmed that they were. With a conscious effort to be polite, for he and she often had falling-outs, the student asked could she hoover them up before they got trodden into the carpet. Helen responded with a shout of 'Yes, Sir!' and several "Sieg Heils!".

The house had an almost permanent smell of garlic because garlic was added to every communal meal prepared by five of the six students; and because the two garlic crushers were added every day, and fished out every evening, to and from the stockpile of used plates and cutlery soaking in stagnant water in the kitchen sink. When the preparations for this evening's food had descended to the point where mayonnaise was being rubbed into each other's hair, the student withdrew to his own room. Through a pair of good headphones left behind by a previous tenant, he listened to the radio whilst writing long letters to the people back home. When music from the neighbouring rooms interrupted the music playing through his headphones, he knew it meant that the rest of the house had eaten and were preparing to go out drinking. This ceremony of noise, accompanied by an almost constant rattle of water rushing through the pipes of his room, always lasted an hour. Never more. Never less. When the house was empty, signalled by the slamming of the front door, which made the framed picture of his skydiving brother rattle against the wall, he knew he could venture from his room, eat something, and start to unwind. If he was relaxed enough he would try reading a book, or start writing an essay. But book-reading wasn't possible tonight. After a while, he tried to sleep, but he couldn't sleep. His nose bled, just a little.

The rest of the household returned after midnight, four of them drunk, four of them sober. All but three accidentally trod broken biscuits into the carpet. The group was not particularly noisy except for their many sharp shushes and one loud shriek. One of them was sick on the lavatory seat.

The sick was still there at noon.

The Landlord

Sprawled in a red leatherette armchair, his head cocked backwards, his hooded eyes looking down, he refused to give a rent book and he offered no contract to sign because he is, he says, a man of his word. "Just a handshake and a deposit and a month's advance rent will do." Then he lectures his catch on rent and property values, the only topics that interest him. They interest him because they are important. He knows they are important because the price of property is mentioned on the news bulletins almost every day, and because there are property programmes on almost every television channel almost every day. Every day the price of property increases, even on the days when lazy journalists scream that the market is heading for a fall. And when the market does fall, the rare small falls of one week or one month or one half-year are more than made up for by the inexorable gains of the next.

"Did you know you can pay a million pounds for a small box bedroom in Westminster?"

The catch can't and won't because he doesn't have a million pounds and because he isn't an idiot. The landlord puffs three times in quick succession on a thin cigarette, a recent affectation which he thinks makes him look clever. (It is his tragedy and his comedy that he could never look clever). He says: "Do you know how I decide the rent?". He smiles slowly at the shrugged shoulders and talks head-noddingly about inflation and "the customary ten-percent".

Uncomfortable on a wooden fold-away chair, the catch (who in time would lose his deposit for it was a point-of-honour for the landlord never to return deposits) glanced at the large television to the right of head-nodding man. The sound was off but the picture was blaring, a property programme to be followed by a crime show and a Karaoke contest, the Unholy Trinity of British Television Culture.

"I chose you," says the landlord, "because I know your job is safe at the university."

He brags he works there himself, "You know", and that he is not a lecturer, nor would he ever be one "even if I had a degree."

A protracted pause.

He says: "It was different in my day. I was never given the chance."

Fat lips suck on a thin cigarette.

Holborn

He was born in the North and schooled in the Midlands and he continued his life journey South by taking a job as an executive for a publisher in London. He was helped to the job by a friend who worked for the company. They had met on an undergraduate working holiday on the East Coast of America. The London offices were in Holborn. The starting salary was several thousand pounds above the national average but this was not enough for the young man to live in London, so he rented a room in a shared accommodation unit in a traffic-choked town to the West of Twickenham. Each working day he caught the train to Waterloo. The trains had plastic seats, six abreast without armrests. Some days he managed to get a seat. The train, which started out at Windsor, in the long winter shadow of the Queen's castle, was usually full by the time he got on board. At Waterloo, he caught a double-decked bus to Holborn. He liked this part of the journey because it took him across Waterloo Bridge from where, looking right, he could see St. Paul's and the river.

In his first week in London, on a rainy day when the roads were fuller than usual, the bus halted briefly in the traffic on the bridge, the driver opened the doors and, to the puzzled amusement of the young executive, almost all the passengers ran from the bus and out into the hard-slanting rain. They ran as if their lives depended on it. All were hoodless and hatless after the fashion of the day. Some held newspapers up to shelter their heads. The young man thought this was strange.

For the first few months, the journey home was less pressured, though the young man soon learned that it was worth his while to catch the 5.25 train. The 5.25 got him back to his accommodation unit within the hour. If he missed the 5.25, he had a forty-minute wait for the next, a stopping train which took nearly thirty minutes more to complete the same journey. So week by week the catching of the 5.25 became more and more important to him. It could almost be said to be more important than his work.

His work was dull and easy and there was very little for him to do. A secretary wrote his letters; a pool of office workers did the actual work itself; so he learned to make work for himself to prove that he was useful. He began to set himself 'targets'. He learned how to schedule and run meetings with other executives who were quite as bored as he. He'd start the meetings with a coffee, and a round-table of chit-chat to put everyone at ease and to fill time. He'd tell the designers to design new 'mail shots', leaflets advertising the company's wares, and he'd get himself all tizzy and busy over the proofs, the printing, the distribution and the delivery of the leaflets. He'd arrange meetings with the subscription services to look again at the subscription renewal forms. He'd tell the telephone sales staff to make five calls more than their daily average which he checked five times daily on his computer. He'd invent new reasons for drawing up charts.

Nine months into the job, he surprised himself when he caught himself running in the rain on Waterloo Bridge.

He remembered the bus sticking in traffic and he remembered the doors opening but he couldn't remember getting off the bus. Hatless, he was running in the rain as if his very life depended upon it.

The year turned and the clock-docking made the evenings light again. The executive was hurrying from the office in Holborn and approaching the road across from the entrance to the Underground. His head was swirling with the nine shades of blue from which he would choose to redraft the company's logo. And that was when he saw the girl. It was probably the first girl he had ever looked at in his life.

The girl was in the road and she was being cradled by a man who was very distressed.

It was clear to the executive that the girl didn't know the man. And it was probably true that the girl didn't know that the man was there, because the girl was too busy dying.

There was a broken bicycle nearby.

And no car. The driver hadn't stopped.

The girl was bleeding from all the wrong places.

There was such turmoil going on inside the girl's body that her eyes seemed to be trying to jump free from her head. The girl was very frightened — very very afraid. Her body started to shake, horribly, but her eyes refused to close.

The executive had done a first-aid course, of course, and knew there was nothing he could do. So he didn't alter his stride. He didn't pause or stop or attempt to look back.

He kept on walking to the 5.25.

ALL
MIXEDUP

The Rugby Player

Last week he scored two tries playing for the second team, having been dropped from the first for missing training and not telephoning in with an acceptable excuse. He could have scored a hat-trick but that would have meant having to buy a £30 jar, which he couldn't afford, so he came up against what he said was an invisible forcefield and he fumbled the touchdown. It was his birthday today but he looked ill. He had hurt his shoulder tackling a man much smaller than himself and was wearing an inadequate sling. It had been fashioned from a crêpe bandage by his girlfriend at home, a school teacher; he had laughed off the injury in the club house where he refused to speak to the physio on the grounds that it would "waste valuable drinking time". For scoring the two tries, which had proved decisive in a closely fought match, his team-mates had got him drunk beyond the point of pleasure so that he only felt ill. He vomited into a bucket and apologised with such mawkish sincerity that everyone felt bad. One of the team-mates, a bearded man known as 'Santa', partly on account of his beard but mostly because he once 'gifted' a score to the opposition, gave an account of last Friday's Gentlemen's Evening at the club house, which involved "two dirty slappers, a can of shaving foam and four fat old forwards who couldn't get it up". Santa said: "It took one of the colts to get the job done properly. You should have seen him come, right over her back and into her hair! The bastard."

"That's jealousy talking," said one of the men.

"I know it is," said Santa.

Everyone laughed.

Love

She was strong (but not as strong as he).
She shouted in public and could be
calculatingly rude.
But that didn't much matter to him.

She frightened away some of his old friends,
and stopped him from bonding with new.
And that didn't much matter.

She put a stop to his hobbies
(and some old fun habits)
and filled the freed space with shoes.

She plucked hair from his ears
(and brows, ouch!)
and that didn't much matter to him,
because being with her made him the man he had always
wanted to be. She took away his restlessness and made him
feel whole.

On the floor they danced navel to bare navel, and head here,
and hands here. And teeth. Holding. And fingers.

Sweat to running sweat.

And it was good.

Country

He was right. He knew he was right. He knew he was right because he knew that he was good. He was good. He knew he was good because he worked always for others and never for himself. That much had been taught to him at school, and that much couldn't be questioned by anybody. He worked always to the best of his ability. He didn't dodge or cheat or lie. But, when questioned about what he meant by 'others', he came to understand that he meant 'country'. And by 'country' he meant 'the Queen'. He never thought beyond the Queen. If there had been time, and he had been able to think a bit deeper, he would have learned that he meant he worked always for his commanding officer. And his commanding officer's bosses. And that he did what he was told, always, because he trusted them to be good. He was a good man, good at his job, doing his good country's work, selflessly. He didn't drink (much). He didn't swear (much). He was good.

So why did they hate him so?

(Hands on guns)

In the desert he started to break down.

Hands on guns.

A long way from home.

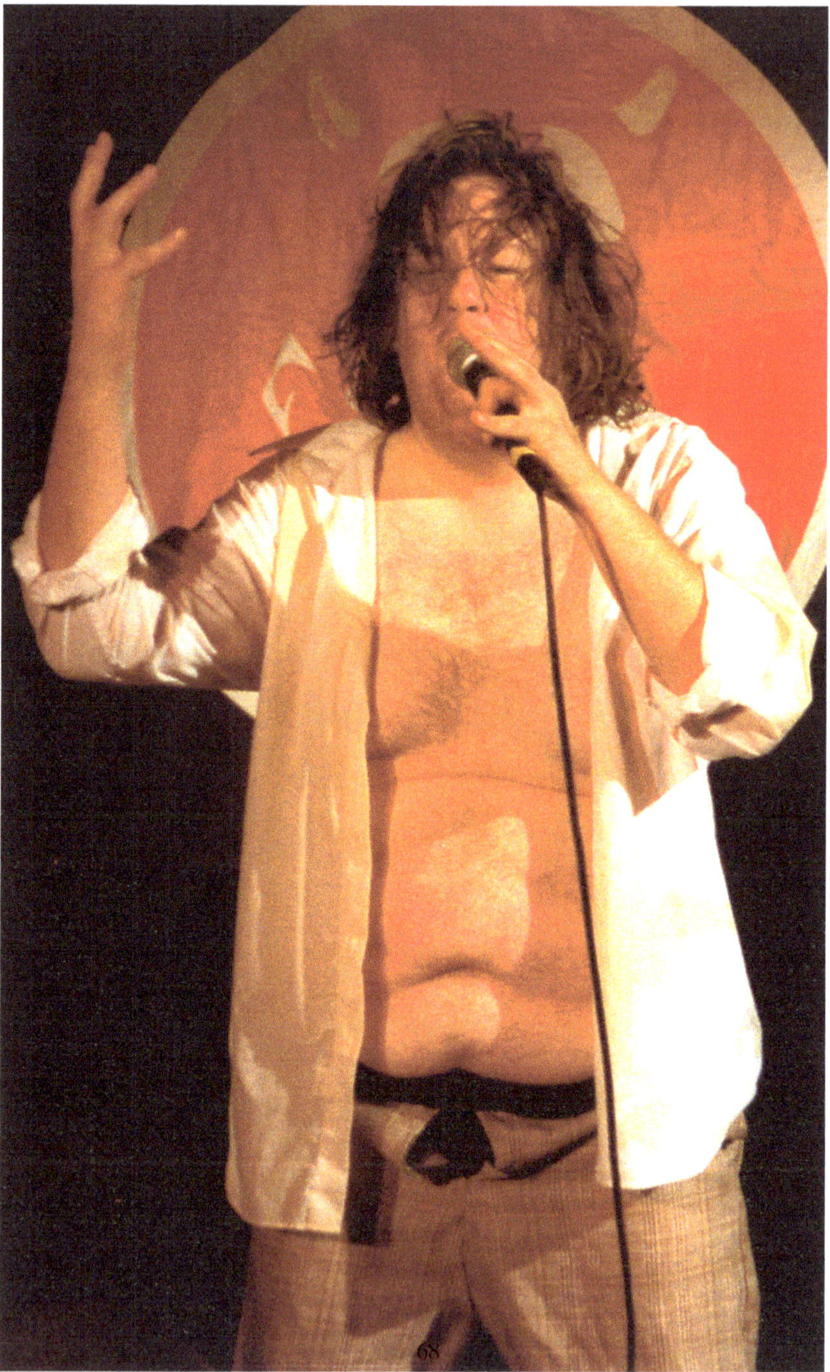

The Old Vic, Nottingham

He took a drink to "say goodbye to winter" and another drink to "welcome in the summer" and, squinting through the spotlight, with one eye more shut than open, he surveyed the laughing crowd. His brain turned over thoughts and lines, but where to start? He finished the black pint with a clean-down-the-gullet pour that made the audience cheer. He raised the empty glass in acknowledgement and stumbled slightly when trying to put it down on a table out in front. The table was hard to reach for a fat man who had been drinking quickly since waking slowly in the short mid-afternoon. A teenager sitting at the table made the pardonable *faux pas* of offering a helping hand to guide the empty glass to the table and the headliner had his victim. "You were worried I was going to spill my drink on your fancy bag! What's in the bag that makes you so protective of it?"

The bag contained cycling gear – a helmet, fleece, luminous vest and a bike pump – all soon worn or wielded by the fat man in exchange for his own leather jacket. "See what it feels like to wear a *man's* jacket!". He tore open the boy's shirt to make the boy look more manly and, with the lad embarrassed but game, he transformed him into *Jeff, Son of Vegas*. "I've been away for so long I can hardly recognise you. Son, it's your *Dad*. I've come *home*. Now come up here and let me see how much you've *grown*."

He taught his son how to be a man, first by beating a heckler at arm-wrestling. Then he tore off his own shirt to beat a bigger man at Sumo. "Son, my back is weak and my time is short. Soon you will have to fight for your father."

He went into the crowd to woo the boy a new mother. The first to catch his eye. "You may hear screams in the night, Son. But it's a sound you'll just have to get used to!"

Now, holding the boy in a mock-tearful embrace, he told of the boy's terrible upbringing, and it made the audience laugh. "Listen to you all *laughing*! We're having a *good time!* We've come *together*. We've become a *community!* And all it took was the public humiliation of this one lad!"

Eighteen volunteers, holding lighters in the darkened room, crowded onto the stage to serve as a birthday cake for Jeff. ("Some of you bugger about with the flame when he tries to blow it out"). And, in a *coup de théâtre*, after an all-together count-up from one to eighteen, the boy was given the gift of his own bicycle stolen from outside the pub. "When you wear out the tyres I'll go out and steal you a car. A Capri! And when you wear that out you can drive your Dad's Jag!"

The show ended with a singing of *New York, New York*.

"Son, you sing and I'll just dance."

The boy sang. And the crowd sang. And the headliner danced.

He danced good.

He danced into a lost world where happiness lived.

Holding Forth

He was fat and rude and loyal. A poor listener. A good talker. He is talking now. I can hear him:

"... in Eton, and it was a great big wedding reception for his third wife, appalling family, all teddy boys with bellies and curly patterns on their shirts. *He* wasn't working class anymore. You go to Cambridge and get an M.A. and you are a gentleman. We had all escaped to the snug in the pub on the High Street and we were talking to this young Earl, not an Earl yet, but a Viscount at sixteen and soon to be a double Earl, 1503 and 1527, a very old family. He had got permission to come out, but having permission from your Housemaster doesn't mean you want to be seen coming in and out of a pub, so he had to be a little sneaky. Schoolboys have to be sneaky to get away with anything, to avoid being punished. He was at a good house and he was very handsome and blond. He wasn't very tall yet but he was a rugger player, in perfect health, heir to two Earldoms. When we went out to the loo, I pushed in front and said to Richard: 'Age before beauty', and he laughed. I said: 'I'm going to let you trade places with me, so you can get to know him a little better.' 'No, No', he said. But I insisted: 'You're much younger. You're much better at it than me. I'm too old for now for *two* Earls.' And we all laughed because it was so ironic.

"We knew that the boy's parents had been multi-divorced and he didn't get on with his father very well although he was his heir. They had great rows but they kept the dialogue going. It doesn't matter who he is, high, low, rich, poor, a boy's relationship with his father determines how he feels about the world, and how he feels about himself, his self-confidence and his sense of well-being, They had a row, years later, when the boy had to put his father into a nursing home in the last months of his life. He lived up on top of this mountain in Gloucestershire and it was very hard to get people to help him. He was going out riding in the car despite being half-blind and with his reflexes half-gone. He was ninety-one for God's sake! The house was still full of valuable pictures and books so he had to put his foot down. His father just wasn't able to go on living there alone. They had this row, but once he got to the home he saw that it was right. He came into about eleven million clear, most of it in the Lloyds of London Holdings which he has been managing ever since. And doing it very well although he never did complete his education.

"Whenever Richard and I met afterwards in Cambridge, we met up at various dinners where they would shower him with honours and he got increasingly old. They really should have put him up for a State Honour, a Knighthood or something like that. He was a very distinguished man. But nobody did. You have to organise that sort of thing but nobody ever did. Philip was very fond of him. One of the last times I met him, he was coming out of Senate House with a new gown on. He was eighty-nine years old, and I was across the way in front of Heffers, or the University Press Shop as we now call it. I'm standing there waiting to cheer. I'm wearing my tweed jacket and my tweed cap, my usual bag and stick, and I shout: 'Well done, Richard! Well done!' And he smiled and came over and shook hands. He's on Edinburgh's arm. Edinburgh said: 'Is he a friend of yours?'.

"Richard says, 'Yes, he's a very old and very good friend.'

"Edinburgh says 'Would he like to give some of his money to the campaign?'

"I said: 'I'm afraid, Your Royal Highness, that I'm constitutionally incapable of flushing my money down somebody else's overdraft.' The university was in the red by four or five million a year. 'Well, that's honest anyway,' said Philip. 'I quite understand. I wouldn't do that with my money. Of course, I don't have any money.'

"I said: 'Well, you seem to manage.'

"He laughed and said: 'Are you coming to dinner?'

"I said: 'I've often accompanied Richard to dinner but if Richard couldn't find a relative for this occasion I'd rather not barge in.'

"Richard said: 'Unfortunately, my family have not followed me out of the working class and are not really presentable.'

"I said: 'I'm presentable but I'm not family. And besides look at my waistline. Do I really need another meal?'

"We all laughed.

"I took my chauffeur and his wife down to St. James's Palace for the Air League Party, of course. My chauffeur is ex-RAF. It was what we call a 'Works Outing'. We had a good time. Good food and drink. Philip came along and said: 'Oh, you again', and he called me by my surname. And he said: 'What's that in your buttonhole?'. I was wearing the purple and gold rosette of the Monarchist League.

I said: 'It's the Monarchist League.'

"He said: 'What does that do?'

"I said: 'It supports you, your wife, your family, and most of the Monarchies in the world.'

"He said: 'Most?'

"I said: 'I personally draw the line at the late Emperor Bokassa.' Do you know who the Emperor Bokassa was? He was a self-styled African emperor and a detested well-known cannibal. Edinburgh laughed. And said: 'We like to draw the line at him ourselves.'

"Another time, down in London, I had dinner with him and we always tease. That's how old sailors and soldiers of that generation are. My father and your father. The way they show affection to their male friends is to tease them. Is to rag them. With him, he likes you to get your rag in first so that he doesn't look brutal when he gives it back. He's done it for as long as I've known him. Our conversations are always funny and open. I remember saying to him once, after I made a very funny but perhaps too cutting remark, 'I do apologise. I'll have to be more careful with my rejoinders.' And he said: 'No, no. Best thing about you, really. I can't think of any other value.'

That's how he is with everybody. Sometimes it looks like a gaffe. On that occasion, he said: 'What's going on in Cambridge? The first issue of the Varsity this year, which I don't ordinarily see but someone kindly sent me one, I'm on the front cover as the World's Greatest Racist?'

"I said: 'I saw that and I should have written to you. When you go on a Royal Visit you smell a lot of fresh paint, and thank goodness none of you are allergic to it. And you are all pretty healthy. When you came into this high room, freshly repainted for your visit, they had taken the scaffolding down but someone had forgotten to replace the white-light fixture.

The wires were hanging down from the ceiling. You came in, and you always like to make a joke to relax everybody and to lower the tension and the tone.'

"He smiled and said: 'You understand me better than I understand myself.'

"And you came in and said: 'Well, it's obvious you've had an Indian doing that'.

"He said: 'It was the first thing out of my mouth. I knew instantly I'd have to pay for it.'

"I said: 'I understood perfectly. I wish I'd written to them and I wish I'd dropped you a note as well. There are fourteen years between our ages, but when I was a little boy, and when you were a little boy, when little boys were allowed to play they played either cops and robbers or cowboys and indians. That was the game. You didn't need any props. You could make the gunshot sounds with your mouth.'

"He said: 'Yes, I played all those games.'

"I said: 'Your mind works rather fast and, like lots of people, your mind works faster than your mouth.'

"He looked at me unsure if this was meant to be a compliment. I said: 'You obviously meant to say, 'You've had a cowboy in to do that' But cowboys and Indians are so connected in your mind, because of all the childhood games, they are phrases that go together, that instead of 'Cowboy' you said 'Indian'. Furthermore, the piece was written by a man called Harriman. It may have looked like an attack on you, but what it really was was a job application for *The Daily Mirror*. And, in fact, he has now got his job on *The Daily Mirror* and he's been crowing about it to everybody. It wasn't personal.'

"He said: 'It felt bloody personal.'

"I said: 'I know. I should have written.'

"He's a charming man. He's charming to everybody, but in his own way, funny, witty, outspoken. He's himself, partly because he can afford to be, The Queen can't. He is her human side that can be shown to everybody. Her really human side she keeps to herself except on certain private occasions or when she's at the track or with her close old friends."

The Bookseller

She turned the sign on the door so that it read 'Open'. Then she sat behind her front desk and waited for the arrival of the F.C. and the F.C.B., the F.F.S. and the F.C.A. These acronyms amused her on the quiet mornings of which there had been rather too many of late. The acronyms always came in the same order. First in was the F.C., which stood for the 'First Customer'. They would come into the shop, nod a polite hello, walk around without really looking at anything, then they would leave. Today's F.C. was the rarest example, a schoolgirl. She nodded a polite hello, walked around without really looking at anything. Then she left.

Next in was the F.C.B. or the 'First Carrier Bag', a sometimes hopeful but mostly expectant and often rude type who arrived with a bag of books they wanted to sell. The books were always, *always*, absolutely worthless: ghost-written memoirs of pop singers and sportsmen, and mass-marketed fiction of the kind that gets fly-postered on bus shelters. "No, thank you. No. No, really. No, not even as a donation. No. No. Goodbye."

Then in would come the person who implied, and who some-times said, "For Fuck's Sake" when taking an immaculate cultural treasure off the shelf and looking at the price pencilled inside. If only the F.F.S. could know the work and the cost involved in finding and saving that beautiful book, to the sale price of which had to be added a percentage of the property rent and insurance, the business taxes and the profit.

This run of visitors concluded with the First Customer *Actual*, the F.C.A. Usually it was one of the bookseller's regulars to whom she had made a weekend phone call from a book fair far away, having found the book during the dealers' careful preview in the quiet moments before the paying public had been let in. "It's V.G. Fine. Yes, Fine. I know. I know. Off-white but unsunned. It jumped into my arms".

The bookseller hadn't yet worked out the acronymous pattern for the rest of the morning, mostly because the flush of pleasure from making that first sale to a valued customer, and sharing the customer's honest delight in the purchase, meant that she was in no mood for silly games for the next few hours, until the drudgery of the F.C.B.s began to wear her down: "A first edition doesn't mean it's valuable. If you think you can get that price for it on Amazon then sell it on Amazon." A 'Like New' copy of the book had been listed (in error or in mischief or simple blind stupidity) for two hundred and forty-nine pounds. "No, I'm not going to give you two hundred and forty-five pounds for a modern B.T.F."

B.T.F. meant 'Bashed To Fuck', an in-joke among collectors and dealers. She hadn't meant to say it out loud.

The door was slammed. The desk papers jumped.

Towards the end of the day, the bookseller got a phone call from a man she knew who did house clearances. He said, "I might have something for you. Do you know anything about someone called Auden?". He pronounced it 'Owden' as in 'Audi'. "A small book of poems with his name written in the front. It's probably his own book."

"Is it in good condition?"

"Not very. The front's a bit bent. It's got some letters stuffed inside."

"Letters written by Auden?"

"Hang on ... No. Sorry. They're letters to a 'Wynston', or something, from somebody called Christopher."

She shut the shop early. For the second time that day she felt alive. She sang Old Testament hymns as she drove eastwards into the dark. Auden's own copy of his poems? With letters to him from Christopher Isherwood? Possibly. Very possibly. Oh, can it be true! She drove not for the money but for the joy of finding. In forty miles' time she would know. She would be holding the book. For a day or two the book would be hers, hers to have and to hold. His hands. Her hands. Their hands. Then she would sell the book to someone of her choosing who would love it as she did. A rare book. A real book. A book that had lived and which was lost and was now found. It would live again.

The Suitcase

They had been friends for years, having met at an exhibition of the younger man's photographs. The older man, better educated and better connected, gave freely of his own knowledge and experience to improve the younger man's art. They met twice weekly for tea and cakes at the older man's Edwardian apartment furnished with original art sun-protected by velvet curtains. They never met outside the apartment, partly because the younger man rarely rose before the afternoon, and partly because the older man never left his apartment after dark. Inside, the older man would show off his latest purchase, bought with self-earned money and love, whilst cultivating the younger's quiet taste. For his part, the younger man listened also to the older man's complaints of the pains of ageing, stifling yawns which went politely unnoticed, and he gave the occasional small gift of thanks. One warm fresh autumn Thursday, the older man asked the younger to take a suitcase to the paper recycling plant. "It's packed so full I can hardly move it." Truly it was a heavy suitcase, blue canvas, made in the era before fixed wheels and trip-wire handles. "Could you possibly empty it for me, and bring it back? I have mince pies for tea."

The suitcase was so heavy, in fact, that a workman at the recycling plant, bored with a colleague's long-continuing prattle, said: "Excuse me, John. I'll give that lad a lift."

Together they heaved the suitcase to the top of the steps above the sky-open bins. "What the hell is in it?"

Resting the case on the metal rim of the bin, the young man unzipped it and out poured a continuing run, a paper waterfall of pornography.

The workman winced.

The Bucket

Scientific knowledge has always depended on the social interest of the ruling class. Thus, with the race to the moon won, the real scientists were marginalised and their funds redistributed to the jokers and to the military, because the small men and women had taken over, over there and over here, and the only thing that small men thought worth investing in were investments that paid cash dividends now. So, instead of colonising other planets, which included growing moss and atmosphere on Mars, which had been planned out by real scientists like Carl Sagan, and which was in reach when I was in my infancy, science was reduced to a kindergarten game of growing mustard seeds on shuttle flights tightly leashed within Earth's orbit. The jokers grew rich telling us that coffee was good for us, then bad for us. Chocolate was good for us, then bad for us. Wine was good for us. Then five new years of paid research told them to tell us that wine was bad for us. The rising temperatures meant that mankind had warmed the planet. The falling temperatures told them that mankind had warmed the planet. The record high numbers of polar bears meant, to the New Scientist, that polar bears were becoming extinct. In this time of dead science (whilst doffing a cap to communication technology, my sweeping has its limits), in a show of strength, and a mission accomplished, which saw scientists punching the air in triumph live on TV, they sent a bucket to one of Saturn's moons. They said it was a probe but it was really just an empty bucket. And, without a child to play with it, it just sits there in the sand, making castles in the air of bombast.

A Song for Christmas

The man had worked in the sciences all of his adult life. At the end of his first month's work, and every month thereafter, he put a good part of his pay into a pension scheme. The pension funds grew until he retired. And now retired in the salt-air city of San Francisco, where he'd lived and worked all of his adult life, he set off to spend his money in Europe. He'd never before been to Europe, but a bit of Europe had been to him, or rather to the Grace Cathedral, where he had heard the Vienna Boys' Choir sing and, against all instincts bred into him, he surprised himself by allowing himself to be moved. It made him feel that he somehow had 'missed out'; that he had wasted a life spent with wires. His response was to stop going to the cathedral for Sunday Morning Mass. That was fifteen years ago. He did so miss the Morning Mass.

The first stop on his European adventure was Vienna. He'd read on-line that the Viennese could be cold, and they could, but the visit went well. He heard the full choir sing three full services. The singing and the services straightened his spine, put a bit of bounce back into his step, and exercised muscles to the right and left of his mouth that had grown weak. His jowls no longer sagged with the full weight of their skin. In Vienna, he played the role of 'good tourist' and cultivated a taste for rich chocolate which he used in small nibbles as a sweetener when drinking black tea.

From Vienna, he travelled to Karlsruhe, South-West Germany, for a film festival in a real old cinema with a giant curved screen. He was surprised to see the city streets lined with cigarette machines. He was shocked by the sight of people smoking. For a few days he developed a psychosomatic cough. In Baden-Baden, he spent an expensive evening listening to an American soprano. Her voice transported him back to times before he was born, when he held a loaded shotgun to keep the crowds back when he freed the slaves.

From Germany, he crossed borders to visit the upper village in the low Italian Dolomites where his father's father was born. He didn't linger long because there were too many watching faces - he didn't feel very safe - but he found the family name carved into the stone of the bench by the Sycamore. He took photographs and donated money to the church. He bought a fourth-hand car for four times its worth (he didn't mind), and he drove it to Rome for eight times the cost of a train ticket (he didn't mind). In Rome, he re-connected with his childhood by visiting the mother called St. Peter. He had thought it over. On the whole, she had been good to him. He lit candles, said prayers and made promises which he would keep. In the quiet contemplation of prayer, with the image of the bones of dead Saints fresh and somehow refreshing in his brain, he recalled his father's words that "Nothing is impossible if you put your mind to it." And it came to him that he should visit England. England at Christmas Time. Carols in Cambridge. King's College Gothic. Surely nothing could be better than that?

He arrived in Cambridge and found the city to be pretty but car-busy. In bed at his hotel, though it wasn't really a hotel, it was a private house subdivided into extra bedrooms and wearing the mantle of a hotel, he read Dickens, and re-watched *A Room With a View*.

He awoke on Christmas Eve morning. It was cold but the central heating was on. The metal radiator was hot to the touch. He'd read that the doors to the chapel opened ninety minutes before the start of the service, so he decided to get there "a full-round-hundred" early to soak up the atmosphere and to get a good seat. He'd never before had to arrive so early for a service but this was the grand finale, a special occasion. He breakfasted (picked at), showered (sort of) and dressed into his best clothes, including a red cotton shirt he'd bought in Vienna. On the three-quarter mile walk to the Chapel, he cleared his mind of all worldly and selfish thoughts in a meditation method he'd been doing for years. "Our Father, who art in Heaven". (My God, the chapel looked good in the fog, carved stone touching the sky).

The gates to the college were guarded by a man in buttoned suit sleeves, a purple cloak, and a bowler hat. A thought passed of 'taking a photo', but the business of worship came first.

The guard stopped him.

"I beg your pardon?"

"You can't come in,' said the guard smiling. "We've closed the doors."

"The doors?"

"Got the word through. You can't come in. All full up."

"I could stand at the back. I've come a long way."

"The doors are closed."

The guard smiled. Pleased with himself.

The man walked away. Hurt. He walked around the block, looking for another way in, and followed a footpath over a river bridge until he came to the back gate of the College. There was still an hour before the service started. But the gates were locked and spiked and too high to climb. He went back to the hotel.

At lunchtime, hungry, he went looking for dinner. He was looking forward to eating his hurt away with an English Christmas Dinner of roast turkey, black fruit pudding and ham.

"You can't come in here, Sir," said the youth in a white shirt and apron inside the Green Man pub. There was no one in the pub. No customers. Just staff in white shirts.

"The sign says 'open'?"

"The bar's open, if you want a drink, but the restaurant is closed. Unless you've booked? We don't open till one."

"Booked?"

"If you haven't booked we can't serve you."

"But there's no one here?"

"It's the rules."

"I don't really need a full dinner. Could you ask the chef to cook me some chips? I can sit here."

"No, Sir. Sorry, Sir."

The boy in the white shirt walked away.

The Old Man

STROUD NEWS
DURSLEY
TESCO

The old man's wife died and, because the old man was an Englishman, he didn't know how to grieve, so he turned inside himself and went a little bit crazy. In losing his wife, he lost everything that meant anything to him so, from now on, he kept everything that came to him, including newspapers, junk mail, old cereal packets, carrier bags, everything in fact. He hoarded it in orderly piles around himself and, when the sitting-room was full, he branched out into the other rooms: the bedrooms, the scullery, the hallway, the kitchen, the garage.

The seasons turned and turned again and, one day, when looking through the kitchen window, he noticed the sunlight on the branches of the trees. Root-still, he stared at it for hours, his mind feasting on the subtle changes of spectacular colours. He watched the light as it moved across the garden.

In the evening he went shopping, and bought pads of good paper and packets of soft pencils, and he began rising earlier from his morning bed so he could study and draw the sunlight on the garden. Like all Englishmen, he had been encouraged to draw almost daily when he was a child and, like all children, he had loved to make artworks from every possible raw material. But when his age had barely reached double figures, he had been discouraged from any involvement in art. Art, to the English, is an infant pastime. Young days and young minds are filled instead with rotes and schedules.

Regretting a life stripped of the pleasures of creation, the old man redoubled his efforts. He taught himself afresh by looking, thinking, working. In the mornings, he would try with his pencils to capture the light in his garden, and he would follow the light, at given points throughout the day, to end the day on top of a hill from where he could see the sun set over the flood-plains of the Severn.

One night, after a meal of roast vegetables and a good Sicilian wine, he was reaching forward from his armchair to mute the noise-boosted advertisements on television, and he knocked over a pile of glossy sheet articles torn from Sunday magazines. Flopping open in front of him was a painting in blue, a woman as seen by Matisse. He stared at the colour and he stared at the form. He greatly admired its simplicity.

He worked now to make his work colourful and he worked to make his work simple.

He cleared the clutter from the sitting-room, from the bed-rooms, from the other rooms, the hallway and the garage, and he burned it all in bonfires on four successive Thursdays.

The final Thursday bonfire was used to make charcoal, ash-less wood cooked within a homemade kiln.

Soon he was creating white light and life from black lines.

Eighty-two

She was eighty-two years old and she didn't give a damn, a phrase she used often. She lived with her only daughter, a pensioner herself, in an ugly town on the south coast of England. The older woman's eccentricities, which included wetting herself at the dinner table, partly out of necessity and partly provocation ("I don't give a damn") were tolerated because everyone thought she was rich. They thought she had money stashed away somewhere, and they thought the money would come to them when she died. The old woman did nothing to dispel this rumour. She gave her two sons, three nephews and four grandsons, small gifts of money here and there, five pounds and ten pounds and twenty-pound notes. She never gave anything to the girls. She liked to boast of the time, years ago, when, in a moment of largesse, she paid for her eldest son to go on holiday to Africa. She paid for the flights. She paid for the hotel. She even gave him spending money. She told this story over and over, nodding all the while, awed by her own generosity. The source of the myth surrounding the old woman's wealth, was the fact her grandfather founded a wine bar that grew into a chain, with links in all the better working class towns, green and red glass-fronted bars where drunks filled their bellies and supped themselves dry.

In the 1970s, the woman dated a Bahraini prince, and jilted him for a ride back to England on the plane carrying Bobby Charlton and the England football team. Charlton and the team had played an exhibition match in the dictatorship of Bahrain. The old woman had liked it in Bahrain, with its private beaches and dry Gulf air, but Charlton's name was 'glamour' and that meant giving it a go, even though Charlton was a married man and not interested at all. In the cargo-hold of the plane bringing her back to England was a gift from the Bahraini prince, a parrot, green-backed and gold. The woman taught it to speak. The first words she taught it to say were 'Bobby Charlton' followed by a choice obscenity which made the woman laugh.

"It only needs some seed and a place where it can shit," she said to the guest at the dinner table.

"Oh, Mother, really."

The parrot could be relied upon to add colour to all social occasions which, in the life of the old woman, were confined almost entirely to festivals on the Christian calendar, gatherings that were always well-attended by family members turning blind eyes and spouting false words.

"You're looking lovely, Mother."

One day, a doctor was dressing the old woman's legs which had become spoiled with wet sores that were refusing to heal. The drugs he'd prescribed were not working. With some apprehension, he suggested lacing the sores with maggots because maggots would eat away the infection. The woman did not attempt to reply. Her silence spoke of indignation. "I'm not a corpse yet," she would say when re-telling this tale over and over at every family gathering.

In an attempt to ease the tension, in a tone adults reserve for prammed children, the doctor made a remark or two at the famous bird. It rarely spoke in the presence of professional men. It ignored his entreaties. When the doctor had finished his duties and packed his bag, and had his hand on the front door, he said a polite farewell to the old woman, and was letting himself out, when a loud voice behind him said:

"Fuck off!"

He turned around to see the old woman looking at the bird, and the bird looking at the old woman.

The old woman laughed.

The Enthronement

Maureen lived in a single-storey house of wood and stone on top of a high hill that overlooked an ancient city. A short walk from the edge of her garden, with its croquet lawn and crocus beds, a covered verandah and creeping vines, and she and her guests — for she always had guests — could look down on the city circling out from the Mediaeval Cathedral. The Bishop, a small single man, had yielded to temptation and fallen from grace. His successor was to be an immensely tall married man who had fathered five children and who stood no nonsense. The new Bishop's first decree, off-the-record-but-make-it-so, would be to ban the unemployed from attending confirmation classes. "They can come back when they have made something of themselves."

Maureen had patronised the Cathedral for the last forty of her seventy-four years, ever since she moved to the area to build her hilltop house of wood and stone. She had sung at public services from the public pews in a piercing vibrato that made the boy choristers grin and which caused the music master to curse, audibly. In later years, when Maureen's voice softened, she took on the role of an unofficial tour guide, opening up the building's closed treasures to more than the privileged few. Doors marked 'private' were respected as 'private' only if she thought there was fair reason for exclusion. She polished the circling tower stones with her feet. She dusted fragile flags of remembrance with her breath.

Though Maureen had only recreational training as a dancer, she once lit up the Cathedral's triennial festival of Arts with a three-woman dance in the Greek style, a bold display of bare feet, bare-ankles and bare legs. Inhibited dignitaries watched through closed eyes and clenched teeth. She gave up ballet soon after her seventy-third birthday, but still attended two public and two private dance lessons weekly and was sufficiently proficient in line-dancing, ballroom, jazz-dancing and tap for there to be no more certificates for her to win. Her only gripe was the insufficiency of men — the difficulty of finding suitable partners. She had a suitable partner though for the Enthronement of The New Bishop which was proving to be the social event of the year. The announcement that it would be attended by three members of the Royal Family meant 'open' tickets were limited to two a parish. Maureen, in her hill-top parish, was annoyed that her ticket hadn't yet arrived. It distracted her thoughts and used up mental energy she reserved for higher things. Her partner for the event was to be a young man newly graduated from university. He was, by his own estimation, a playwright of much promise. A reading of his unperformed plays satisfied Maureen that his claim was not without truth so she had admitted him into her inner circle. This meant he could stay at her house whenever he wanted to. They had met on a six-week Cathedral course on the sources of the Bible, readings from rejected Gospels and the Dead Sea Scrolls. He was keener and livelier than the rest.

"Wear your tweed jacket to the Enthronement," she said looking down from the hill. "It goes nicely with your fair hair. Ordinarily tweed wouldn't be suitable for such a formal occasion, let alone one with royalty in attendance, but your black jacket is too loose at the shoulders. It is better to look good than to look right. And get your hair cut."

"What will you be wearing?"

"My furs, of course. And my necklace." Her necklace was a commission in gold of a 747 aeroplane in the shape of a cross.

"It is important to remember man-made tragedies," she said. "Loss is a part of human existence. It is Nature's Law that everyone will lose the one they love, but unnatural losses should be remembered and despised."

"Despised?"

"They go against God."

The day came but the tickets had not come. "What are we going to do, Maureen?"

"What a silly question," she said, looking him up and down. "Give your shoes another rub with the polishing cloth. But, before you do that, help me on with my coat."

He helped her with her coat. The cream fur was so rich and so warm he could almost hear it purr.

She said: "I'll wait for you in the car."

The car was a red Triumph Spitfire, open-topped and tuned to a rev-roaring satisfaction. "Get in," she said to the hurrying young man. "If it is anything like last time, they'll have closed the streets."

And they had closed the streets. Policemen were everywhere, on rooftops and at checkpoints. England's foreign policies of the day had created a domestic climate of state overstaffing, state-paid overtime and fear.

"Get out of my way," she said to the policeman at the first check-point. His hands had asked her to stop. His mouth tried to ask for identification.

"Get-out-of-my-way," she said again. He moved out of her way.

She drove on. On through the business district. On through the closed shopping streets. And on to the second checkpoint: "I haven't got time for your nonsense. I've got an Enthrone-ment to attend!", she said with snap and purpose to the uniformed man with the outstretched hand. He stood aside and waved her through.

When she was out of sight from the checkpoint guards, she turned left and drove up a pedestrianised street empty of everything but the chewing gum dropped daily by insecure schoolgirls.

"Can you hear it sticking to the tyres?"

"What?" said the boy.

She spun the car on a right angle and drove up a tight lane that took them to the wrought iron gates of the Cathedral close.

They were locked.

"What are we going to do now?" asked the boy.

It was nothing that a few sharp bursts on the car horn couldn't fix. These caught the attention of the gatehouse guard. He came out of the office and was charmed by a cheerful: "Andrew, sorry to trouble you but we were told to come this way by the man on the blockade. Do let us in."

He returned to the guardhouse and pressed the button that opened the gates. They were in.

"How did you know his name was Andrew?"

"I didn't."

The cathedral towered above them, Cotswold gold in the mid-morning sun.

"We can't park here, Maureen. Not in the Cathedral close. There isn't any space."

"You surprise me," she said to her guest. "I didn't think you were sheep-trained only to look at white lines."

She parked the car in a large empty space. Its bumper pushed up against the very stones of the Cathedral.

"Maureen?"

"I'll go first. You walk in four or five paces behind me. If I'm asked for a ticket I'll say you've got it. If you are asked, you say I've got it. They'll be too flustered to think on their feet, particularly if there is a crowd behind us."

A crowd of ticket-carrying patrons, many in new suits and new hats, were filing in beneath the carved sandstone arches and through the double-oak ticket-checked doors. The air was heavy with the scent of lilies. Maureen wiped smiles too wide to be sincere from the faces of the pinstripe-suited door-guards by blanking them with condescending waves of her jewelled left wrist and by saying, in a very firm voice, the single word 'No!'. This had the desired effect of stopping them from asking to see her ticket. Unchallenged, she walked into the nave. Her guest had almost as much luck. When asked to produce his ticket he said: "My mother has it. She's the lady up in front." The one walking at pace towards the altar. They let him in.

When he caught up to Maureen, she said: "I'm surprised but glad they let you in, but it was bad form of you to say I was your mother. Your mother, I am sure, is an admirable woman but she is not me. I'm a patron and a friend and you are my escort, perhaps even my badge, but you are not my son."

"I'm sorry."

"You are too young to play with untruths - especially in a Cathedral. Now, where should we sit?"

All the seats were numbered with numbers that corresponded with numbers on the tickets. Flocks of ticketed patrons were checking aisle numbers and seat numbers. There was a lot of 'excuse me, please' and people wearing smiles as they stood up to let others brush past.

"Ah, yes," said Maureen, spying one of her two favourite words: 'Reserved'.

She ducked under a barrier and into the reserved section at the front, near the altar. "Now, do we want an aisle seat? Or shall we sit in the middle?"

Then she noticed that the first three rows had leather cushioned seats and were much better than the rest. And that settled it. She entered the front row pew from the left at the same time the first of the Royals entered it from the right. They met in the middle. Tradition dictates that Royalty are the last to take their seats in everything except religious services. Her Majesty's momentary surprise to be sharing the pew with Maureen, and Maureen's guest, was eased by Maureen giving her a polite nod, a half-curtsy, and by handing her a service booklet: "Your Majesty".

Her Majesty took the booklet, smiled, said 'Thank you', and sat down. Maureen sat down next to her.

A deacon who knew Maureen well by sight, and who always came off worse when trying to discipline her, had a hand on his forehead and was quietly banging it into a wall. Another deacon who had seen Maureen in the seat next to Her Majesty, strode forward at a pace which slowed to a complete stop as he got near because his thoughts had caught up with his actions. He knew it would be a mistake to try to intervene. He backed away and said nothing.

The aisles behind Maureen filled with royalty of lesser rank. The organ, which had been playing an air so quietly as to be almost subliminal, announced with a flourish that the service was about to begin. Maureen stood up. The whole congregation followed her lead and stood to attention.

The choir entered singing. Gold boats of incense swinging.

Glowing inside with an immense feeling of satisfaction and happiness, Maureen decided to roll back the years and give thanks to The Lord by taking on the organ, and by taking on the congregation, and by taking on the choir as she had in times of old. During the singing of the processional hymn, her voice rang with such piercing authority that the number of accidentally dropped service sheets could almost be counted as rhythm. The music master cursed but Her Majesty was charmed by the sight passing before her of sixteen small singing-boys, their cheeks flushing with rude joy.

301108
DUFFICEY

The King

He always had delusions of grandeur. When he was a boy playing cowboys and indians, he was never a cowboy or an indian. He was always The Chief. He stood still as the others fought around him, shooting and scalping and war-crying. He stood impassively still. Noble. Still. Arms folded. He passed Judgement. His word was Law. When the battles grew to World War, he was never a soldier, never a Tommy and never a Nazi. He was The General. He stood still, impassive, as the others fought around him. He didn't crawl on all fours, or tear his clothes on the bramble bush. He didn't jump into the river to splash the girls. And he didn't take part in the rescue missions to free the prisoners. But he took the glory, as was his right. He was always the last man standing.

And now in an age when he is not so old, but not so young, and with a body broken down, failing daily and dying soon, the now bed-ridden man is having his last Christmas. The nurses have been in to empty and to clean and to bring cheer. There's a crown on his head, gold paper from a cracker. He is trying to remember the joke. One of the nurses read out a joke, something about a split infinitive, and it didn't make sense. He can hear the noise of televisions. He can always hear televisions. He can hear the television in the room to the right of him, and he can hear the television in the room to the left. In the room to the left is a man who was a master of a Cambridge College. He is happy to be resting in a room next to a man of such good standing. Standing. Standing? He tried to remember the last time he stood on his own two feet. Aided or unaided? He couldn't remember the last time he stood up. How long have I been here? What is this room? What is that noise? Then everything started to go white. Is that me? I can see myself standing tall as all around me fall. War cries. War crying. Why is he crying? That stone hardly hit him. And it wasn't a very big stone. I'll tell Johnny that his brother is too young to join in. If Johnny insists then Johnny will have to go.

From his propped position on the bed, on pillows that are changed daily, he catches a reflection in the glass of a painting hanging on the wall. The painting is of his father. He can see that his father is wearing a crown. And he tries to remember his father's crown. Was it gold and quite plain? Was it covered with jewels? He couldn't remember the jewels. He squints and tries to lean forward, but he can't lean forward. He squints again and catches a glimpse of his own face. And then it all makes sense. The crown is not on his father's head, it is on his own head. He can see his own crown reflected in the glass. He tests this by moving his head gently to the left and gently to the right, and the crown in the glass moves. And that makes him feel good. He remembers the Coronation. All those flags and happy smiles. And people lining the road twenty deep. "Hoorah! Hoorah for the King!" He tries to wipe away a tear, a good tear made from pleasure, but finds that he can't move his arm. Where are the servants? The servants have been neglectful of late. I will give them a dressing down. He tries to press the bell but his fingers don't respond. Where are the servants? The Queen? Is she weeping? She needs to be told. And bring the children. Bring the eldest first. Bring Andrew. Andrew needs to be told.

Also published by Buffalo Books

The Moving Picture
Boy Gallery

Tim Dry
Falling Upwards

Ken Russell's
Dracula

Becoming
Ken Russell
by Paul Sutton

John Francis Lane
To Each His Own
Dolce Vita

camerajournal@hotmail.com

www.ingramcontent.com/pod-product-compliance
Lightning Source LLC
Chambersburg PA
CBHW061105100726
47911CB00012B/401